D0239632

characters created by
lauren child

But I AM an alligator

PUFFIN

Text based on the script written by Bridget Hurst

Illustrations from the TV animation produced by Tiger Aspect

PUFFIN BOOKS
Published by the Penguin Group: London, New York, Australia,
Canada, India, Ireland, New Zealand and South Africa
Penguin Books Ltd, Registered Offices: 80 Strand, London WC2R 0RL, England

puffinbooks.com

This edition published in Great Britain in Puffin Books 2012
001 – 10 9 8 7 6 5 4 3 2 1
Manufactured in China
ISBN: 978-0-718-19523-6
This edition produced for the Book People Ltd,
Hall Wood Avenue, Haydock, St Helens, WA11 9UL

I have this little sister Lola.
She is small and very funny.
One thing Lola loves is **dressing** up.
"This is my favourite **fancy** dress
costume and I'm not ever NEVER
taking it off," says Lola.

Then Lola says,
"Did you know **al-li-ga-tors** live in
swamps and rivers
where they are very
difficult to see?

That's because they are
ca-moo-flarged.

And, you know, **alligators** lay eggs,
not babies.

"And sometimes they grow BIGGER than even our table!" says Lola.

"So you see, Charlie, alligators are really very interesting. That's why I am going to wear my alligator costume ALL the time."

So I say,
"ALL the time, Lola?"

And she says, "Yes, Charlie.
I'm not taking it off ever! NEVER!"

When Mum takes us shopping, Lola says,
"I want to eat what **al-li-gators** eat."

I say,
"I don't think they eat frozen prawns, Lola."

But Lola shouts, "Oh, they absolutely do,
Charlie! Alligators LOVE frozen prawns!"

And I say,

"Shhh, Lola. Everyone's looking at us."

At the park, Lola is STILL wearing
her **alligator** costume.

Marv says, "Have you asked
her to take it off?"

So I say, "A **gazillion**, million times, but she says she is going to wear it FOREVER!"

And Marv says, "Well, she can't wear it to **school**, can she?"

And I say, "NO! She **can't** wear it to **school**!"

"Of course I am going to wear it
to school," says Lola.

And I say, "I really don't think it's such a
good idea. Won't your friends think wearing
an alligator costume is a bit strange?"

Lola says,
"No, Charlie. I think they will all want
alligator costumes, too.
Especially when I do my **talk**."

So I say, "YOUR TALK?"

And Lola says,
"Yes, Charlie! We have to do a talk in
assembly tomorrow.
It's called 'All About Me'."

Then I say,
"But you are NOT an **alligator**, Lola.
Don't you think it would be better if
you tell the whole school about YOU, dressed
as YOU? You could tell them about...

"... how you like

drawing...

and how you

always hop into bed...

and how **pink milk**
        is your favourite
   and your best."

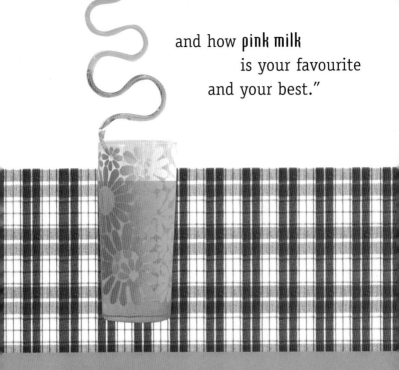

        Lola says,
"That would not be very interesting. Everybody
    already knows I like **pink milk**!"

And so I say,
    "I could help you
    with your **talk**, if you like."

But Lola says,
    "I do not **need** any help."

At assembly the next day, Lola says,
"My name is Lola,
and I like **dressing** up.

At the moment,
I like **dressing** up as an al-li-g̲ator
because it is my most fa𝐯ourite
costuᴍe and it is my best.

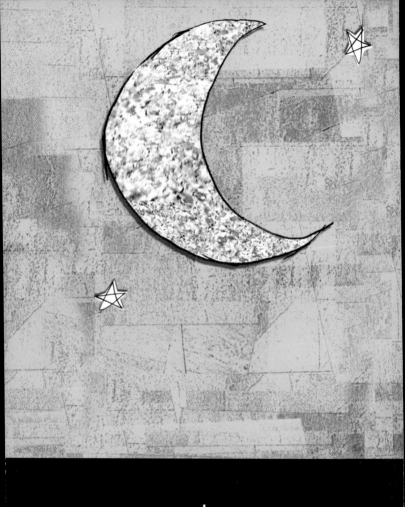

"I used to like **dressing**
up as a Spanish lady.

"... a doctor!

Or a caterpillar...

And the whole school says,

"Wow!"

who turns into a **butterfly**."

Lola says,
   "I love **dressing** up,
because I can be whatever I want to be...
      and that is my **best**."

Everyone cheers. And I say, "Well done, Lola!"

The next day,
Lola is not an **alligator**.
She has whiskers, pointy ears and a tail.

Lola says, "Meow!"

And I say, "Oh no."